To Tom, Ella and Ethan – my own crazy team
Love you always

Chapter One

Today is the day. D-Day. And in all honesty, I reckon it's going to be the worst day of my life – so far.

I watch Mum and Richie from the safety of my bedroom window. They want me down there with them. They want me to do the right thing, to get involved and show them that I'm happy with this sweet new arrangement.

But I'm not happy, am I? In fact, I'm far from it.

From up here, I shoot dirty looks at Richie's soppy face as he unloads his boxes and stacks them up on our driveway. So many stupid boxes. How much stuff has he got? I can't stand how smug he looks as he loops his arm around Mum's waist and kisses her cheek. He looks like he already owns the place, and Mum too. And look at Mum – giggling like a girl. It turns my stomach. So pathetic.

Just behind them, Kayla is holding a smaller box. She looks out of place standing there – too pretty and perfect to be leaning on our rough, crumbling wall. I see Kayla's nose wrinkle, her lips pouting with boredom, then her eyes move up to meet mine.

We are locked together in an icy stare. I don't want to break my gaze away, but I have to. This is Kayla Roberts after all. She's not just older than me but also one of the most popular girls in school.

Maybe this is a bad day for Kayla too. Does she really want this to happen?

Mum is making such a huge mistake.

Mum really wants me to like Richie. It's painful to watch. Mum's eyes go all wide and pleading and she starts coming out with all the reasons why her boyfriend is so good for us.

"He makes me laugh," she says. "He's so kind. He just wants to make us happy."

I don't agree. For one, he doesn't make anyone laugh apart from Mum – and she's the type of person who finds adverts for toilet roll funny. Any normal person would find Richie loud, annoying and think he tries too hard. As for his kindness, OK, he might be all right to Mum as far as I know. But what man tries to muscle in on a woman who was just doing her job? Mum told me that she had been caring for Richie's sick dad and she and Richie had begun to get close. She told me that Richie was "struggling". He had lost his wife years ago and his dad's death had brought back memories of that. Mum keeps going on about how kind and sensitive Richie is, like I care. He isn't being so kind and sensitive now, is he? Breaking up our home, ruining everything. I bet Dad doesn't see him that way.

And the last reason – he wants to make us happy? God, don't even get me started on that one. That's the biggest lie of them all, because if Richie Roberts wanted to make us happy, he would leave us alone.

I'm sorry. I probably sound all bitter and twisted, and maybe I am. I can't help my feelings. I hate upsetting Mum, but the fact is I will never like Richie and it's not worth pretending.

I have a dad already. And he's the one who should be coming home now, clasping my mum's hand and beaming up at me.

Not Richie.

Mum is making a special dinner. She never normally cooks, so this meal is bound to go horribly wrong. I feel like staying in my bedroom for the rest of the evening, but I know this will cause more trouble than I need. So I slip downstairs and watch as Mum fusses around in the kitchen. I avoid the living room, because I know Richie and Kayla are in there. Already taking over space, watching what they like on our TV. Laughing far too loud. I really can't deal with it.

I lean on the door frame, watching as Mum moves around the kitchen, humming softly to herself under her breath. She's pretty, my mum – everyone says so. She is tiny and cute like a doll and has delicate features. I look nothing like her. I'm all Dad.

It makes me feel a bit sad that Mum's only cooking like this now. Normally she just sticks a pizza in the oven or mixes up a pasta dish from a jar. I've never seen her chopping up ingredients or weighing things out. In fact, I didn't even know that we owned a set of scales. This is all for Richie. This is all to prove to him how perfect we are – which is another stupid lie. Mum never did this for Dad. It seems unfair somehow. A red-hot fire burns in my belly.

Mum looks up, finally spotting me. Her eyes widen. I guess she's surprised I'm there at all.

"Hey, Poppy!" Mum says. "Want to help? I'm making a Thai curry."

I shake my head and tell her, "I hate curry." She knows this.

Mum's cheeks turn pink. She pushes a strand of her dark hair away.

"I know. But it won't be that hot." She sighs. "It's Richie and Kayla's favourite. I want to help them settle in."

Of course she does. Because it's all about them.

I nod, not wanting to say any more, and slink away from the door. I think Mum watches me for a bit. I can feel her eyes burning into my back.

I sit on the stairs, trying to ignore the noise from the living room. I could go in there. That's probably the right thing to do, but I really can't face it. Suddenly I feel small and pathetic. It doesn't feel safe to be in my house any more. It's all changed.

I reach for my phone and dial Dad's number. If I can just speak to him, I know I'll feel better. I want to feel normal. I want him to tell me it will be OK.

My ear presses against the phone hopefully. Waiting.

But of course it just goes to voicemail again.

"I want to propose a toast," Richie says. He's standing tall, his glass raised. "To new beginnings."

"New beginnings," Mum, Kayla and I chant.

I am staring. I'm trying not to. But it's so hard seeing Richie sitting there, in Dad's chair. Richie doesn't fit it properly. He's too loud. He's too smiley. I want Dad back there. Dad never tried too hard. He could make people laugh without even trying.

Richie catches me looking and winks. I look away, cringing.

Next to me, Kayla is playing with her food. She doesn't look impressed but is saying nothing. She takes up loads of space at the table and her elbows keep knocking mine. I'm getting irritated – I swear Kayla's doing it on purpose.

I slam down my fork. It makes a louder sound than I intended. Now everyone's eyes are on me. Richie raises an eyebrow. Mum glares at me.

"I can't eat this," I say simply.

Kayla sighs dramatically and mutters, "Seriously?" under her breath. I ignore her. I'm not going to let her wind me up in my own house. Just because Kayla's older and pretty doesn't mean she can act all superior.

Mum looks over at me. "Please try," she says. Her voice is firm. Her teeth are set in a fake smile, but I know she's angry.

I stare at Richie. He's still smiling. This just makes me feel even more annoyed.

"I hate spicy stuff," I say to Mum. "You know that."

"It was a treat for Richie and Kayla," Mum says. "It's Richie's favourite meal." Her voice is cool. "I thought it would be nice to make them feel welcome on their first night here."

In other words, she means, *You're doing a pretty lousy job of welcoming them.*

"Come on, Poppy," Richie says to me. "Just try some." He raises his fork, as if to tempt me. His stupid giant mouth of perfect teeth is still grinning at me. "It's really lovely," Richie adds.

I push my plate away. "I'm sorry ..."

But I'm really not.

Mum's eyes are glinting. "Poppy," she says. "Don't do this."

"I'm sorry I can't join in with your 'happy family dinner'," I hiss. "It just doesn't taste right to me."

I push away my chair and stomp out, nearly tripping over Kayla's legs, which are far too long. She mutters something like "sorry", but when I look up at her, her eyes are cold.

Kayla takes a mouthful of the food, turns to Mum and says, "This really is lovely, Kat."

I see Mum beam and Richie reaches over to squeeze Mum's hand. They look at each other with soppy faces. It turns my empty stomach.

As I walk out of the door, I hear Richie say, "She just needs time ..."

Time? He has to be kidding. They could give me all the time in the world and I would never accept this.

I slam the door loudly behind me and crash out of the house.

Chapter Two

I have nowhere to go – nowhere interesting anyway. I end up just walking to the shops and spending the last of my money on a chocolate bar and some crisps. Then I try to call Dad again. He's not great at picking up his phone, which used to drive Mum mad. Now he's even worse because he works all sorts of hours as a van driver. But I get that.

Even so, I could really do with talking to Dad right now. I find myself swearing under my breath as I listen to his voicemail kicking in once again. I know he's busy. I know he's got to start his life over since Mum threw him out. But even so ... it would be nice if he called me back sometimes.

I don't bother leaving Dad a message. Instead, I fire out a text, hoping that he might read it during a quiet time.

Miss you. It's horrible here. Can I see you soon?

I last saw Dad three weeks ago. We kept changing when we would meet because he had to sort out a new flat and then got this new driving job. I was pleased for him. At least he's working now. Mum was always moaning about Dad "sitting around and not doing anything", and then she would moan about him being "out with his mates all the time". To be honest, she has always been pretty mean to him. Dad could never win.

When Dad and I last met up, we went to the burger place in town. It was OK. Dad had lots of questions about Mum. He didn't seem too happy when I told him Richie was moving in – Dad's entire mood changed. That's the thing with Dad – normally he's funny and chilled and one of the best people to be around, but when something upsets him he becomes quiet and sulky. It can be frustrating. I hate seeing Dad upset. I know things weren't perfect between him and Mum – I'm not stupid. But surely they could have worked harder to fix it? It just doesn't seem right that they gave up so soon.

I shove the phone back in my pocket, feeling annoyed I couldn't speak to Dad. Then I set off on a walk. There's really nothing around here, just the shabby row of shops and a playing field where people walk their dogs. It's pretty lame. Even the park is small and neglected, with battered swings and a slide caked in muddy footprints. I don't think young kids use it any more.

I walk down the path that snakes past the field. It's already fairly cold, so I pull my jumper sleeves over my hands to keep them warm. My head is fizzing with different thoughts. I wish I didn't feel so angry, but it's hard not to when everyone is trying to mess up your life.

I never asked for any of this.

I just want my family back.

As I turn the corner, I see a group of kids sitting on the benches by the football pitch. There are about eight of them from school, mainly girls but a few boys too. I can see Lia

Armstrong clearly. She is standing up, and her long, glossy dark hair is whipping around in the wind. I don't understand how she can be out here in just that tiny top and ripped jeans. She must be freezing. I see she's laughing – her standard fake "I'm so happy" laugh that seems to echo across the whole school. One of the boys reaches up and touches Lia's arm gently. The other girls are laughing too.

I turn my focus back to the path and keep walking. I hope that they don't see me. I really don't need their attention today.

I'm rounding the last corner on my way back to the house when my mobile begins to buzz in my pocket. I dig it out and know it's Dad before I even look at the screen. My heart leaps. I imagine him in his tiny bare bedsit, sitting on the second-hand sofa he's just bought. He'll be tired, I bet. He'll probably be drinking a beer to help him sleep.

"Hey!" Dad says, his voice light and cheerful. "I missed your call."

I smile. I don't say, "You always miss my calls", because I know how busy he is right now and I don't want to stress him out.

"Dad!" I say. "Can I see you tomorrow?"

I'm really hoping that he will let me. I'm happy to sleep on his scruffy sofa overnight. Anything is better than being stuck in the house of smugness for days on end.

"Ah – Pops ..." Dad says, breathing hard. I wonder for a moment if he's smoking again. "I'm really sorry but I've got so much on at the moment. I'm working a lot and I still have to pick up some bits for the flat."

Disappointment stabs at me. I can't fight it.

"Can't I just pop over for a bit?" I ask.

"I don't think I've got time, sweetheart," Dad says. "Not tomorrow."

He only lives half an hour away. A bus ride. He wouldn't even need to pick me up, but I know there's no point in arguing.

"How's things there?" Dad asks. "How's Rich Richie?"

I can hear the bite at the end of Dad's sentence. He hates Richie as much as I do – calls him a "flash git" and moans about him taking Mum away from him.

"He's ... He's the same ..." I say. I'm almost at my front door. I look across at the living-room window. I imagine Richie sprawled on the sofa, his arm around Mum, his hand clutching the TV remote. Already in control. Richie was like this before he'd even moved in. It'll be worse now.

"Is your mum OK?" Dad asks, his voice soft.

"I guess."

"Ah ... that's good."

We both know it's not. Not really. We want her happy with us again.

"I better go, Dad," I tell him. "I'm home now." My hand is on the door.

"Poppy ..." Dad hesitates. "What about the weekend? Saturday? I'll take you to a match, yeah? Just you and me? Fancy that?"

My skin prickles with excitement. Normally Dad says he can't afford to take me to games any more. He knows it's my favourite thing to do.

"Really?" I ask. I'm trying to contain my excitement. "You can sort that?"

"Really," he replies. I know he's smiling.

I end the call feeling brighter. At least now I know I'll be seeing Dad soon. We can watch the football, have a laugh.

It'll be like old times again.

Chapter Three

It seems so wrong to come down to breakfast and find Richie there at the table, his size almost taking over the room. He grins as I walk in.

"Hey, Poppy!" Richie says. "I was about to give you a shout. You don't want to be late."

I frown and give him my "yeah, thanks for that" stare before getting myself some cornflakes. I don't need Richie's help getting ready in the morning. I'm used to doing it on my own. Mum always leaves before six to start her shift at the nursing home.

Kayla strolls in a few minutes after me, already munching on a piece of toast. I can't help glancing over at her. She looks so good. If I put that sort of make-up on my face, I'd end up looking like some kind of weird clown. But

Kayla seems to get it just right. Her cheekbones shimmer as she moves across the room and gives her dad a peck on the cheek. I bet she doesn't have to watch endless make-up tutorials on YouTube to get her look right. She's just one of those girls who know how to do it without having to learn.

"I'm going now," Kayla says brightly, then she looks over at me. "You coming?"

I pause for a second. I never thought Kayla would want to walk to school with me. I'm just a Year Nine for a start, while she's in Year Eleven. Not only that, but I'm a Year Nine with acne and bad hair. I can't imagine we'll have much to talk about. But I ram a spoonful of cereal in my mouth and nod. Anything is better than being left alone with Richie. He is bound to start talking again, trying to be my new best mate.

I can't face that.

"Are you not going to eat your breakfast?" Richie says, and gestures to the bowl that I've just dumped in the sink.

"Obviously not," I say.

"Most important meal of the day, you know."

I shrug. I'll be fine. I don't bother to tell Richie that I have a Twix in my school bag.

"You ready, then?" Kayla asks, and waltzes out. I follow her, breathing in her sweet perfume as I trail behind.

"Dad's all right really," Kayla says, "once you get to know him. I mean, he drives me mad sometimes too, but he could be a lot worse."

Really?

We're walking down the main street towards school. Kayla is talking to me while also stabbing out a message on her phone. I can't text and walk at the same time. I'd just end up crashing into something.

"I don't need another dad," I say, then realise how sulky it sounds.

Kayla sniffs and says, "To be fair, I don't think he's trying to be. He's not like that. He's actually pretty much OK most of the time."

My eyes scan the ground. I have no reply to this. Of course Kayla's going to feel differently.

This is her dad we're discussing. But it doesn't mean I have to like him.

"Your dad's still around, isn't he?" Kayla asks lightly.

"Yeah, of course." I am defensive, wondering what bad stories Mum and Richie have been making up about Dad.

"OK," Kayla says. "Calm down. I was just asking. Does he still live round here?"

"Yeah. The other side of town." I glance up at her and see that she's looking at me now. "He has a really nice flat," I tell her. "Proper modern. Hopefully I can stay there soon."

She nods, half smiles. "That's cool."

"We're going to the match on Saturday," I say. "He's getting tickets."

Kayla's back on her phone now, losing interest. "Yeah? Dad said something about you being into football."

Into it? She doesn't know the half of it. I love football so much I'm almost obsessed. I've been watching games since I was tiny. It's something

20

that makes me feel truly relaxed and happy. How would Kayla understand that?

"I can't wait. It's an important game," I tell her.

Kayla pauses. Looks at me and then back at her phone again. "Good," she says. "That's good ... Poppy? Is it OK if I go up ahead? I have to meet someone."

I shrug. Sure. I guess I couldn't expect her to want to actually walk into the building with me.

Kayla smiles and half waves. "Cool. I'll see you later."

Then she sprints off, like she can't get away fast enough.

When I walk into my tutor group, I know something is about to kick off. Lia is standing by Emily Westcott's desk. I can see from Emily's face that this is not a good thing. Emily is one of the shy girls in our year. She doesn't have many friends and tends to get left out of stuff. Today, Emily looks awkward and stressed – her cheeks are bright pink and her eyes look watery.

Without thinking, I stride over. Lia sees me and grins.

"Hey, Poppy," Charlotte says, one of Lia's best mates. "Have you heard the latest?"

Charlotte giggles and hands me a phone. "Have you seen this? It's so lame."

I look at the screen, not sure what I'm meant to be looking at. There is a screen grab of a conversation between Emily and a boy in Year Eleven – Jamie Stokes. All Emily has said in the conversation is "Hey – you OK?"

"See, desperate Emily has been hitting on my boyfriend," Lia says smoothly. She turns to Emily. "That's not good, is it?"

Emily shakes her head. "I didn't. I swear. I know Jamie from swimming. I was just asking about—"

"Nah ..." Lia's voice is like ice. "I'm not listening to that. You don't hit on other girls' guys. This is a private message. It's obvious what you're doing."

I hand the phone back to Charlotte and say, "To be fair, this doesn't say much."

Lia turns her attention to me. "What do you mean?" Lia asks. "It's clear. She just private messaged him."

"So what, if they're friends?" I say.

I can't see the issue here. Emily looks at me and flashes me a "thank you" smile. Something uncomfortable stirs inside me.

"I can't believe you're taking her side," Charlotte hisses at me. "I mean, I always suspected you were a snake, but now—"

My cheeks flush. I round on Charlotte. "I'm no snake!"

"Sounds like you are from here!" Charlotte replies.

I turn to Lia. She is standing there with this stupid smug look all over her face. I don't know why Lia has to start arguments like this. She is always kicking off over something and it's normally pathetic and irrelevant.

"Lia – you said you dumped Jamie last week?" I ask, trying to keep my voice calm.

Lia shrugs. "It's off and on. So?"

"So ... He's not your property," I say. "You can't claim him like this."

Lia laughs. It's deep and hollow. "Oh, I think I can. Jamie knows he's with me and he thinks this is pathetic too. He wouldn't be seen dead with someone like Emily. How do you think I saw the message? Jamie thinks it's sick."

"So why are you worried, then?" I ask.

Lia eyeballs me and draws her mouth into a sneer. "Who said I was worried?" she says. "This bitch just needed a warning. That's all."

I shrug. "It all just sounds a bit desperate to me."

"Really?" Lia says, and laughs softly. She steps away from Emily's desk, drawing closer to me. "It sounds like someone round here needs to check where her loyalties lie. Or maybe they need a warning too."

I half laugh and turn to go to my desk. "I'm done here, Lia," I tell her.

"Really?" she says. "I don't think I am."

Chapter Four

My best mates Daryl and Fliss are not in my tutor group, which is annoying. So I normally sit at the back with Freddie Harris and chat about football instead. I'm still raging about Lia's performance just now, but talking about the weekend's game is helping to take my mind off it.

"You're so lucky your dad's getting you tickets," Freddie says. "It'll be a tight match, but it should be a good one."

I like Freddie. He's one of those loud, in-your-face kids that everyone seems to get on with. He's not part of any group; he just drifts between all of us with ease. Plus, he likes football and is funny, which is a winning combination for me.

Freddie nudges me just as the bell is about to go.

"You've totally rattled Lia's cage," Freddie says. "She keeps flashing you evils. If looks could kill, you'd be dead on the floor by now."

I look up and catch Lia's glare. She is definitely pissed off at me. I hope she'll calm down – she normally loses focus pretty fast.

"How come you got involved?" Freddie asks. "Emily isn't a friend of yours, is she?"

"No," I say. "But even so, I didn't want her getting grief when she didn't deserve it. She only messaged a guy. It's hardly a reason to hang her."

Except it is in Lia's crazy-arse world.

And now the noose is around my neck. And I can feel it getting tighter.

Freddie shrugs. "Yeah, I'm sure it'll all blow over." He grins at me. "Just focus on something else. Like the football!"

I nod. Suddenly excited. "Yeah," I say. "I can't wait. It seems so long since Dad and I last went."

"I heard tickets are really hard to get," Freddie says, "especially this late on in the week."

I know this already. It's always hard to get tickets for this game. Our team, United, are playing City, our biggest rival. It's the first time the two teams will play since City were promoted into the same league. Last time we met, United lost by two goals, so it's really important that we win this one to prove a point. We really are the best.

"My dad will sort the tickets," I say.

Dad has loads of friends. He knows people who know people. He's bound to get the tickets easily.

"You're so lucky," Freddie moans. "I'd kill to go."

"My dad is the best." I smile back.

At least I have something good to look forward to.

By lunch it has got around that I've upset Lia and Charlotte. This isn't exactly good news. Daryl grabs me in the lunch queue and almost squeals in my ear.

"What did you do?" Daryl asks. "The rumour is you've been a complete snake."

I frown at Daryl. I like her. She is one of my oldest mates, but she loves drama and gossip. Plus, to be honest, she should know me better than that.

"I'm no snake," I say coolly.

"Well ..." Daryl replies, extending the word for effect. "That's not what's being said."

We walk over to where Fliss is sitting. She's the most chilled out of the three of us and very unlikely to have noticed the rumours. Daryl sits next to Fliss and nudges her.

"Lia is after Poppy," Daryl says.

Fliss looks up from her sandwich. She seems bored. "Really?" she says. "Why?"

"Poppy took someone else's side."

"I didn't," I say, and slide into the seat opposite them. "I just stuck up for Emily. Lia and Charlotte were having a go at her for nothing."

Daryl sighed. "Emily has been texting Lia's ex-boyfriend, Jamie."

"She sent him one message!" I say. "It's crazy."

Fliss shakes her head. "It all sounds pathetic to me."

I laugh. "Exactly!"

I look around the room. As usual, Lia and her group are sitting right at the back. I can hear them laughing from here. Lia has her back to me. She is sitting *on* the table and leaning over to talk to someone. But Charlotte is facing me. She sees me looking and holds my stare for a moment.

Then Charlotte smiles.

It's not a nice smile.

I switch my attention. Across from us I see Kayla is sitting with a load of kids from her year. She looks a bit bored and is picking at her lunch. Next to her is Jamie, Lia's ex. He leans over and says something to her and she laughs.

Interesting, I wonder if they are friends, I think.

"Poppy, are you even listening?" Daryl is talking again, flapping her crisp packet in front of my face.

"No – what?" I say. "Sorry."

"I was just saying to Fliss, you need to watch out," Daryl says. "I heard Lia wants to get back at you for making her look silly."

"I didn't make her look silly! I just told her what I thought."

Fliss snorts and says, "That's making her look silly. You have to agree with everything Queen Lia says, don't you know?"

I shrug. This is stupid. I don't have time for it.

"Just watch yourself, that's all," Daryl warns me. "Lia and Charlotte can be pretty mean if they want to."

"Bring it on," I mutter.

I'm not scared of those two losers.

*

By the end of the day, I am fed up of the whispers and rumours. I think about confronting Lia once the bell rings but decide she isn't worth it. Knowing Lia, she'll soon find some other poor mug to hassle and will forget all about me.

Anyway, I have more important things to focus on. As soon as I pull my phone out of my bag, I see that I have two missed calls.

The first voicemail is from Mum. She's talking really fast and tells me that she and Richie are "going out tonight" to celebrate him moving in. I can't help rolling my eyes. She says that she has made me and Kayla some stew and left it in the slow cooker. Mum says this like it's some kind of treat, but she knows stew is something else I can't stand.

But at least I don't have to face an evening of smug Richie spread out on our sofa, pretending to show an interest in my life. Perhaps for one night the house will feel normal.

The second voicemail is from Dad. It's faster. Blunter. Asking me to call him back.

I do so straight away as I walk home from school, not bothering to wait for Daryl and Fliss. For once, Dad picks up on the first ring.

"Pops!" he says. "How was your day? Sorry to call – I couldn't remember what time you finished."

I smile to myself. I have finished school at the same time for years. It's really not that hard.

"I was thinking ..." Dad says softly. "I really need to pick up the rest of my stuff soon. Do you think you can find out when would be a good time?"

My heart tightens. I'm not even sure Dad has much stuff left in the house. Mum did a pretty good job of clearing it all out in plastic bags ages ago.

"What stuff do you mean, Dad?"

"Well ..." he says, and breathes hard. "I was thinking ... it's only fair ... I paid for that TV. Half of that bloody furniture."

He sounds so angry. I recognise the tone. He gets like this sometimes – when he's been down the pub too long or had a stressful day. I can hear the slur in his voice. I know he's been drinking again.

"Shouldn't you be talking about this with Mum?" I ask.

"Oh, I tried that. But she won't listen. I'm guessing she's much too busy now."

"Well ..." I pause, feeling awkward. "She is working long hours."

"Stop protecting her, Poppy." Dad sighs heavily again. "Just tell me, how is it fair? How? She kicks me out. Then moves her new fella in within months. What am I left with? Eh?"

I can't answer that. The truth is I don't know and I really hate being asked this question.

"Dad ... I ..."

He snorts. "It's OK. I don't expect you to understand."

"But I do, Dad," I tell him. "I do ..."

We're silent for a moment, and it hangs between us. I grip my phone, unsure what to say next. I thought Dad had been coping better.

"Are we still going on Saturday?" I ask nervously.

"Saturday?" Dad repeats as if confused, and then, "Ah yes, Saturday. Of course. I'll be there, Poppy. I can't wait."

"Me neither."

"I love you, Poppy." Dad's voice is so thick. "I love you so much."

"I love you too, Dad."

The call ends. I should be excited. But I'm not.

I'm just full of worry.

Chapter Five

Mum kicked Dad out last New Year's Eve. It certainly made the year start with a bang. She didn't say much to me after – just that she couldn't live a life of regret and that Dad was making her unhappy.

I really don't think she considered how I felt. She never asked me.

OK, I wasn't stupid and I knew things weren't perfect between Mum and Dad. I had to live amidst the constant arguments and rows after all. Mum was always getting frustrated at Dad for not "holding down a job for more than two minutes" or "drinking too much" or "not helping around the house". I guess I could understand that it wasn't easy for her. But I also knew that it had been hard for Dad too. He had loved his job on the building sites and it was hardly his fault that his back problems meant he couldn't do it any more. I knew that Dad went to the pub as an "escape". Having a drink relaxed him and made him feel a bit better. I know sometimes he went too far, but it wasn't his fault. Not really.

And it wasn't his fault that Mum fell in love with Richie.

It seemed to me that Mum had completely given up on their marriage and Dad had been destroyed by it. It wasn't like that for other people I knew. When Fliss's dad had an affair, her mum insisted that they went to marriage counselling. Fliss's parents are still together now. So that just shows that some things can be fixed. It doesn't have to be thrown away for ever.

If Richie hadn't come into Mum's life, maybe it would've been all right. Maybe Mum and Dad could've worked things out too. If Richie hadn't shown up at my mum's work, maybe it would've been OK. He changed her. Suddenly Mum was like a giggly kid, always texting and making phone calls. It was so pathetic.

I remember the first time I met Richie. Mum was still with Dad then. She and Richie were "just friends" and she brought him over to introduce him to me. I couldn't even believe that Mum would enjoy spending time with someone like him. Richie was so different to Dad. Loud, stupidly over the top and with awful taste in clothes. I looked at his bright orange shirt and literally cringed, but at the time it hadn't mattered. He was just a friend after all. Nothing more.

But then Mum told Dad to leave. Then, weeks later, Richie started to come to the house more and more. It was so obvious, but I didn't dare say it out loud because I was scared that I would make it true.

My mum had found someone else. She didn't want Dad any more.

And she just expected me to accept that.

The first thing I hear when I walk into the house after school is Richie singing. Loud and out of tune. It really grates. I pause for a second at the front door, my key still in my hand, and debate whether I should just walk back out again.

Then Kayla strolls out of the kitchen. She is eating an apple and laughing. She sees me and rolls her eyes.

"Dad's singing never improves!" Kayla says. Then, spotting my expression, a frown creases her face. "What's up with you?"

"Nothing." I slouch forward. "It's just been a stressy day."

In my pocket, my phone buzzes again. I know what it is without looking at it. Lia has set up a group chat completely slating me. It seems it's more fun to have me included in the chat. I could delete myself of course, but I don't want Lia to think I'm bothered by her pathetic tantrums, so I'm trying my best to ignore it.

But it's hard. Especially when people that I thought were OK are joining in, posting laughing emojis and agreeing that I'm "out of order" and annoying. For example, I never knew that Grace Evans thought I was a "stuck-up bitch". I guess it's one way of finding out who your true friends are.

Kayla half smiles and says, "School's grim. I saw you at lunch. You seemed OK then?"

I shrug. "I guess." Then I can't help adding, "You were sitting with Jamie."

"Yeah. He's a good mate. I've known him since we were kids."

In the kitchen, Richie is still singing. I swear it's louder now. I dimly recognise the song. Some sad old nineties tune that my dad loves. The thought makes my heart twist.

Richie shouldn't be singing that.

"Do you know Jamie, then?" Kayla asks.

I dump my bag in the corner and peel off my coat. In my pocket, my phone buzzes again. "Not really. Someone I know used to go out with him."

Her frown deepens. "Really?" she asks, and looks surprised. "I didn't think Jamie had been seeing anyone lately."

"Maybe he kept it quiet," I say.

"No." Kayla shakes her head. "No. I would've known. Jamie's not one for keeping secrets. Anyway, I'm pretty certain he wouldn't have been interested in your friend."

But this leaves me more confused. If Jamie hadn't been seeing Lia, then why was she going around saying that he had? Surely there was a risk she would be found out?

I can't help smiling. Maybe Lia has gone one step too far this time.

Thankfully, Richie stops his noise when I walk into the kitchen. He has made himself some coffee and is standing looking out of the patio windows that lead to the garden. He's dressed in bright blue trousers and a clashing green shirt that's tucked into his waistband. I wonder if he even looks in the mirror when he gets dressed.

"That's a lovely garden," Richie says when I walk in. "In the spring, I'd like to get to work out there. Make it look really good."

I stand behind him. It's fair to say that the garden is a mess. Dad isn't handy like that and Mum just never has the time. All I can see now is overgrown grass, huge bushes and sprawling trees.

"Just think how good it could look," Richie says.

I grunt. "Yeah. Probably."

It would be just like him to show off his skills like some kind of superhero.

I go over to the slow cooker to inspect the stew Mum has left us. Lifting the lid, all I can see is thick brown sludge. I pull a face.

"Where are you going tonight?" I ask Richie.

"There's a new Italian in town," Richie says. "I thought we could try it." He sounds excited, and looking up at him I can see his eyes are sparkling like a big kid.

"Nice," I say.

"If it's good, we could all go there?" he says brightly. "Me and your mum can be the testers."

I nod. *Whatever.*

He walks towards me, his arms hanging awkwardly by his side.

"So ... How was your day?" he asks.

"Fine."

He sniffs. "Any homework to do tonight?"

"Some," I reply, and stare back at him. "You don't have to do this, you know."

41

"Do what?"

"Act like my dad." I pluck an apple from the bowl and take a large bite. "I have a dad already and I don't need or want another one."

I quickly walk out of the room before he can ask me anything else.

I stay in my bedroom for most of the evening. My phone is out on my desk. I can see the messages popping up and I try to ignore them. But it's hard, and I end up reading the constant stream. I think the entire year group, more or less, has been added to the chat. I can see Lia is enjoying playing the victim here. Her first post claims that I was really "aggressive" towards her for no reason and now she's upset because she considered me a friend.

A friend! That's a joke. Lia only ever spoke to me if she wanted something or needed to copy my homework. I've known Lia since primary school and she's always been one of those girls who are nice to your face and then mean behind your back.

This is different. Now she's hitting out at me online. Of course Charlotte backs her up, saying that I'm just an "ugly snake" who probably fancies Jamie too. I snort at the thought. I couldn't think of a worse boy to fancy.

What surprises me is that Emily has been added to the group – after all, this whole thing started because of her. I see that she has replied mid-way through the chat and I hover over her message, convinced that Emily will be supporting me.

Her words are like a punch to my stomach:

Yeah, I reckon you should be worried about Poppy. She's always had it in for you, Lia. Why do you think she got involved in our argument? It was nothing to do with her. Poppy was just looking for a chance to have a go at you.

I blink and take a deep breath. What a bitch. I weighed in. I supported Emily and this is the thanks I get.

I scroll further down. Not everyone has replied. Some people have said it all sounds a bit stupid, but only Fliss sticks up for me properly:

Delete this now, Lia. You know Poppy isn't a snake. Leave this.

Daryl hasn't said anything. This doesn't surprise me. She's always been scared of getting into a fight.

I keep reading the words and my mind is raging. I can't believe Lia could be so petty and that Emily could be so weak. I am stabbing out a reply before I can stop myself. My fingers are working so fast it is like they are on fire.

Screw you, Lia.

Maybe next time you have a go at someone for "messaging" your boyfriend, you should be sure you get the details right. Or was your relationship with Jamie as made-up as this pack of lies?

And, Emily – next time it looks like you're going to get your face slapped, I'll be the one watching with my popcorn.

See you later, losers.

And I switch off my phone before I can see their angry replies.

Chapter Six

Friday morning. When I switch my phone back on, it's flashing with messages. The only ones I bother to open are those from Fliss and Daryl. Daryl's, as I could have guessed, is pretty dramatic:

Pops! What have you done? Lia is raging.

Thankfully, Fliss is more matter of fact. I love her for this.

Wow! You dropped a bomb there last night! Nice one. Bet Lia is pissed.
No worries, she will be stressing about someone else by midday. Meet at 8?

I text Fliss back with a smile on my face. Yes, I'm happy to meet her on the way to school. To be honest, I probably need a mate to walk in with just in case Lia and her cronies are lying in wait for me.

I shower and dress quickly, then go downstairs for breakfast. I am surprised to see Mum still here. She must be going in late. She is in the kitchen and Richie is standing behind her, his arms wrapped around her waist. Mum is giggling like an idiot. There is no sign of Kayla. I'm guessing she took one look at this loved-up scene and legged it.

I roll my eyes. I can't help myself.

Mum laughs and says, "Sorry, Poppy." She slips out from under Richie's large beefy arm. "Did you want me to do you some toast?"

"No, I'm fine." I pour myself a glass of milk, keen to get out of there as soon as possible.

"We had a lovely night out yesterday," Richie tells me, like I need to know. "It was good spending some quality time together."

Seriously? Is he having a dig? I stare at him, trying to work it out. "That's nice," I finally mutter.

"Maybe next time you and Kayla can come?" Mum says softly.

"What? And play happy families?" I say, then gulp the milk. It seems to stick in my throat. "Perhaps I can invite Dad too?"

"Don't be silly, Poppy," Mum says.

"He phoned yesterday," I tell her, watching how she shifts a bit and how her eyes drop. "He asked after you. He always does."

"Poppy—" Mum starts.

Richie steps towards me. "I think your mum finds this difficult," he says.

I laugh. It's a hard sound, almost like choking.

"She's not the only one," I say.

Fliss meets me at the top of my road. We often don't walk in together, because she tends to go in earlier than me. Fliss is one of those types who is academic but doesn't get stick for it. I wouldn't go as far as saying that she's considered cool, but most people leave her alone – probably because she really doesn't care what anyone thinks about her.

In my next life, I want to come back as Fliss.

She smiles as I walk over. "Talk about causing a drama," Fliss says, holding up her phone. "This thing hasn't stopped buzzing."

I shrug. "I'm trying not to look, to be honest." I pause, then add, "So what's Lia saying now?"

Fliss sniffs. "The usual crap. That you're a snake. That you probably fancy Jamie. That you've had issues with Lia since primary school."

"Seriously?" I say. I can't help laughing.

Yeah, OK. There was a time when Lia and I were kind of friends. We are going back a bit here – we were about seven years old. Then Lia drifted away and started being the "popular girl" with the loudest mouth, but I still liked her. There had been no issues at all. I found her mildly irritating at times, but I never said anything.

Well, not much anyway.

I sigh and say, "School will be fun today."

"They will soon be fixated on someone else," Fliss says smoothly. "But I don't get the message you sent. How do you know that Jamie and Fliss weren't dating? She has pictures of the two of them all over Instagram. According to Daryl, they were pretty serious."

I shake my head. "It was just something I heard. Maybe I was wrong."

"Maybe," Fliss says. "But it probably wasn't the wisest move to say that. You know what Lia is like. It's all about keeping up her reputation."

"Yeah, I know."

Was Lia always like that? I'm trying to remember, but it's difficult. Time passes so fast and people become different.

That's the problem with most things. People change and you don't even realise it's happening.

School itself starts OK. I text Dad on the way in, telling him I'm looking forward to the match on

Saturday – because, let's be honest, I need that escape. Then I lose myself in the crowd. I try not to catch anyone's eye – just move quickly to my tutor-group room. Lia and Charlotte are already there, but so is Mrs Vincent, so nothing is said. I spot a few dirty looks being flashed my way as I slide into my seat next to Freddie, but other than that, nothing.

Lia even smiles at me as she passes me at the door.

I nod, not sure what to do next. Should I say sorry? But then again, why should I? She set up the group about me. I just responded. I haven't done anything wrong here. I can feel myself stiffen, my strength building. Dad always taught me to stand up for myself. I'm not going to back down now.

"Morning, Poppy," Lia says brightly. Too brightly.

I smile back. It feels fake and heavy, but I do it anyway. Charlotte grins briefly, but I can see her eyes are as cold as ice. Both girls move off down the corridor in front of me. I walk slowly after them, thinking it's best to stay behind them.

"You shouldn't have said that last night," a voice says behind me.

I turn. It's Emily. Her bright beady eyes blink at me. I feel a flash of anger.

"If it wasn't for you," I say, "I wouldn't be in this mess."

"I didn't ask you to get involved," Emily mutters.

"So what's the deal anyway – were you flirting with Jamie?" I ask.

Emily shrugs. "I've known him for ages. It was nothing. But Lia is obsessed with him. She hates to think anyone else will get with him."

"But were they even going out?" I ask. "I heard—"

"Yeah well, you heard right." Emily cuts me off. "They were barely together. Lia just sees it as more."

Emily starts walking, so I have to gather speed to catch her up. "Emily. What's going on with you? Why won't you say something?"

She half laughs. "It's just not worth it, is it?" Emily says. "If you get on the wrong side of Lia, she makes your life a misery." She looks at me again. Her eyes are shimmering. "So good luck with that."

I pretty much survive the morning. I mean, yeah, a few looks are sent my way, but nothing major. I can deal with that. I'm pretty certain Lia must have moved on to something else by now.

As soon as the lunch bell goes, I dig out my phone and check my messages. I was hoping that Dad would have replied by now, but there is nothing there. I try to ignore the familiar tug in my stomach. I know he's busy. It's not his fault if he can't respond to me right away.

Even so, it would've been good to have heard something from Dad today. Anything really. I just want a sign that I'm still in his thoughts.

I walk into the lunch hall still skimming my messages. We're not meant to have phones out at school, so I'm taking a major risk. If one of the moodier teachers spots me, it will be confiscated for a week or more. The trouble is, I can't help scanning the group chat messages again. There's no wi-fi at school and I've used all my data, so the messages haven't updated in a while, but I can still read the ones sent earlier. In particular, the one that Lia sent just before school started. The words aren't exactly great to read:

Poppy will get what's coming to her.

Why didn't I spot this before? What does Lia mean?

I feel more anxious as I move across the hall, suddenly feeling eyes on me – watching me, checking me out. To be fair, they probably aren't, but that's what it feels like. I quickly grab some food and load my tray, then I go to find Fliss and Daryl. I just want to sit down and keep my head low for a bit. With any luck, Lia's message means nothing at all – just a silly threat sent in the heat of the moment.

I churn over the events in my head. Do I regret what I did? Maybe. It was stupid of me to get involved with other people's arguments. I should've known better. It isn't like I need any more grief in my life. It's always better to keep your head low at school. I knew this, so why the hell didn't I do it?

"You're too hot headed, Poppy," Mum said to me once, calm and concerned. *"Too quick to leap in with both feet without considering the consequences."*

When had Mum said this to me? Was it after the time I let rip about Richie moving in? I had thrown a plate across the room then, called Mum names that I had instantly regretted. Weirdly, Mum hadn't seemed angry with me afterwards. Just sad, like she was struggling to understand me.

That was worse than being angry somehow.

I move fast across the hall and out of the main doors to join Daryl and Fliss in the outside seating area. I don't see until too late that I need to pass Lia and her group of mates. They have chosen to sit on the large table just outside the hall. My eyes flick towards Lia and I can see she is staring right at me. There is no smile now. Just a hard, unforgiving stare.

I look around. The teacher supposed to be on duty out here has been distracted by some Year Seven boys messing around in the hall. He is now striding back inside. I don't want to be hanging around this table too long. Lia is bound to say something, especially with no school staff in earshot.

I rush past, not wanting to stop, not wanting the hassle, but I don't move fast enough. I feel a shove from behind, catching me hard. I stumble, crying out stupidly. My tray crashes from my hands. I stagger, but the momentum takes me. I can't stop the inevitable fall. My knees hit the floor hard; the concrete paving vibrates into my bones. All I can hear is the crazy-loud sound of the lunch tray crashing to the ground.

And their laughter. Actually, that is the loudest sound of all. It cuts through all the rest.

I look up. Frozen for a second. Confused. Who pushed me? It could only have been Charlotte. She is standing right behind me and her hands are held up in a defensive "it wasn't me" position.

But of course it was. I can tell by her smile.

"Aw, Poppy," Charlotte says. "I didn't realise you were so clumsy. Are you OK?"

Lia and the group around her snigger. I don't reply, just attempt to sit up. My cheeks are burning.

"Aw and look," Charlotte goes on. "You spilt your milkshake. What a shame. Do you want some more? I have some here."

And before I can turn, or even shout out a response, her strawberry drink is dumped on my head. It's surprisingly heavy. I can feel the cold sludgy mess dripping down my neck.

I lift my head high. I push away the strawberry froth that is already trickling down my face. I blink hard. I will not cry. I will not give these bitches the satisfaction.

In front of me, Lia is now smiling. And she's holding out her phone.

She is filming everything. Of course she is.

It is as if everything else around me is silent.

Slowly, I stand up. I try to ignore the giggles and whispers from the table.

I pick up my bag and I walk. I don't care that milkshake is still spilling out of my hair. I don't care that my tights are ripped and my shirt is now stained.

I don't care about any of that right now.

I just need to get out of here.

Chapter Seven

I don't know what to do. I just need to get away from everyone. I realise that I am running now, along the empty corridor that runs down the back of the Art block. It's always quieter here. There are some toilets at the end and I fling myself inside, shoving past a group of Year Seven girls who are chatting by the door.

At the sink I run the tap and splash water over my head. I don't care what it looks like. I just want the stuff off me. I grab handfuls of paper towels and scrub my cheeks and neck.

"What happened to you?" one of the girls asks. She is small and thin with hard eyes that seem to be studying me, like she knows what just happened.

"An accident," I mutter, but inside I am raging. *How could they do this to me? How is this right?*

The girl reaches into her bag and pulls out a hairbrush. "Here. Use this."

I smile weakly and thank her, then attempt to drag the brush through my matted damp hair. At least it looks a bit better. But I can still smell the sickly scent of milkshake on me. It's making me gag.

"Are you sure you're OK?" the girl asks, taking back her brush.

"Yes. I'm fine." I grip the edges of the sink, trying to fight the shaking that is taking over my body.

One of her friends speaks up. "Maybe we should get a teacher? Someone to help you?"

"No." My voice is firm. "Please. Just leave me alone."

They file out, muttering under their breaths. Probably wondering what sort of weirdo I am. Who could blame them? I would think the same thing if some milkshake-covered girl with crazy hair ran into the loos.

The silence in the toilets calms me a bit. I take a few shaky breaths and then look back into the mirror. I look so pale. There are streaks on my cheeks where I cried and my skin is red where I scrubbed it. I still can't stand to look at my hair.

Hearing a noise outside, I rush into a cubicle and lock the door. I sit on the closed seat of the toilet, pull out my phone again and look blankly at the screen.

I want to call Dad. I want him to pick me up and make this all better, but I know I can't.

Minutes pass. The bell rings and I can hear the corridor coming alive with noise. But I stay seated, unable to move. I can't face everyone else. Not yet. My stomach twists and turns.

I wait. I don't even know how long for, but I know that it's silent outside. I know that everyone will be back in class, getting on with their day.

And then I slip out of the toilets, find the back entrance onto the playing fields and I walk.

I walk right out of school and I don't plan on going back.

Dad always used to pick me up from school when I was small. It was easier for him to be there, because Mum's shifts were long and unpredictable. Anyway, it soon became our thing. I got used to seeing Dad's smiling face at the gate.

And if I'd had a bad day, he was always there. To give me a hug or to talk about it with me. Dad was good like that. Somehow he always had the right words to make it better.

I remember when I was nine. For some reason, all the girls in class had turned against me. I had been left on my own at break, watching as the others played and giggled behind their hands. I hadn't got a clue what I had done wrong, but I hated the heavy feeling that was pressing in my stomach. It was as if a brick was lodged inside me.

When Dad collected me that day, I told him that I didn't want to go back to school. That I hated it. That I couldn't face it again.

I remember he took my hand and squeezed it in his. We didn't talk much at first. He just led me to the newsagent and let me pick my favourite ice cream. Then, once we were walking home, he began to speak.

"Sometimes you have to treat a bad day like a storm in the sky," Dad said. "It can come out of nowhere. It can sweep you up, turn your world upside down and then, before you know it, it's gone."

"But everyone hates me," I said.

"Nobody hates you, Poppy. How could they? You're amazing. You just have to remember that. The key to getting through a storm is holding your own. Keeping steady. Don't let yourself be swept up in it. If you can show the world that you can get through this, it won't beat you."

"I don't think I can, Dad."

"Of course you can," Dad told me. "You can do anything, Poppy. Just don't be scared. Hold your head up high and ride that wind."

And of course he was right. By the next day at school, the "storm" had passed. My friends were talking to me again. I had got through it.

But this feels different. Today is more personal, more humiliating.

And I haven't got Dad waiting at the gate to help.

The sky is dark and heavy. It looks like it will pour down any minute. I don't fancy getting soaked on top of everything else today, so I decide to head straight home. Mum will be at work, so I'm hoping I will have the place to myself. I just want to get my head together and work out what I'm going to do next.

I realise I've made a mistake the minute I walk in the door. I can hear Richie's voice. It's loud and forceful and it's pretty clear he is talking about me.

"... it's OK, love. I think she's just got home. Yes. Yes, I will talk to her."

I stand frozen in the hall, my cheeks burning. Richie strolls out of the kitchen, his mobile still clutched in his hand. He actually looks a bit awkward as he strokes his chin, his eyes gazing at me.

"Poppy," Richie says. "Where have you been?"

"Why are you here?" I hit him with a question too, hoping it will deflect his attention.

"I'm working from home." Richie shoves the phone in his back pocket. "That was your mum. She's worried sick. The school have just called her saying that they spotted you on CCTV walking out of the building. What on earth is going on?"

I shrug. "Nothing. I just felt sick."

He frowns. "Then why didn't you go to the medical room?"

"It was closed."

"Really?" Richie says. "It's never been closed before and yet it is today? So there were no teachers to talk to? No one on reception?"

I bow my head. I have nothing to say. Not to him anyway.

Richie sighs. "Poppy, what is going on? Has someone said something to you?" His eyes scan my face, my hair. "What on earth has happened?"

"Nothing is going on."

"The school seem to think—"

"This has got nothing to do with you," I shout over him, my anger flaring. What has this got to do with him? It's bad enough that he's standing in my hall, but now he's trying to pry into my life too.

"I'm only trying to help," Richie says weakly.

"Well, don't!"

In my room, my phone is buzzing loads. I scan over the messages quickly, trying not to get too stressed. Most of them are older texts on the group chat. People arse-licking Lia, telling her that they are on her side.

Yeah, of course they are. They are too weak to be anything else.

There is a message Fliss sent at lunch. Asking if I'm OK. Asking me where I went.

Then I start to read the latest updates. I've been tagged in something recently. How did someone even do that? They must have sneaked their phone out in class. It's from Lia – and it's of me.

It's a video. Of me falling to the ground and then sitting, stunned, as milkshake is tipped on my head.

I watch numbly as the likes roll in. People I thought were friends are posting laughing emojis and thumbs-up messages.

I watch as Daryl, one of my oldest mates, someone that I've trusted for what feels like for ever, posts a heart.

I feel like my own heart is breaking.

I phone Dad again. I don't care that his voicemail clicks straight on. Even hearing his bright, upbeat voice helps a bit. I imagine Dad standing with me now, wrapping his arms around me, telling me it's going to be OK. It's just another storm.

He's who I need right now.

"Dad," I croak, once the beep has sounded. "Dad, I need you. I need to be with you. I'm bringing my stuff to the match tomorrow. I just want to stay with you for a few days ... I'll explain when I see you ... But I just need to get away. If there's a problem, call me back ..."

I shut off the call, hoping for once that he doesn't ring me back. I'm hoping he'll be OK with me staying for a while. After all, he's offered it before.

"Pops, you can sleep on my sofa. Anytime. It'll be fun. Like the old times ..."

I smile, still clutching the phone in my hands. This is all I need. Just a bit of time with Dad, some space away from everything. Hopefully it'll all calm down and I'll be in a better place to deal with it.

"I'm not letting you win," I mutter to Lia. In my mind, I can see her, laughing and joking with everyone, happily destroying other people's lives. "I'm not letting you win at all. I just need some time."

It's amazing how much stronger I feel as I pack my small bag. It's almost as if today never happened at all.

I'm going to be just fine.

Chapter Eight

"Poppy," Mum says. "Can I come in?"

I am surprised to see Mum at the door. She used to wake me up all the time when I was small, but not so much now. I guess she just respects my space more. Also, a lot of the time she leaves the house early, long before I'm even awake. It feels a bit weird, seeing Mum's face peer into my room. I cringe, knowing she will be upset about the state of it.

I am laid out on top of my bed, still in my PJs, not ready to go downstairs just yet. I'm trying to read a magazine, but not much is going in if I'm honest. Every time my phone buzzes, I have to check to make sure it's not Dad – but of course it isn't. I can't face reading the endless messages people are sending about the video. I keep hoping it will end soon.

"Richie said you were rude to him yesterday," Mum says, walking over to me.

I don't answer. To be honest, I really don't know what to say. If I admit the reason I came home, Mum will make a huge deal out of it and things will probably get a million times worse.

She comes towards me. Flaps my magazine shut.

"Poppy. What's going on?" Mum asks. "You can't just walk out of school like that. They were really worried about you. They said they were concerned that there might have been a fight."

I know Mum struggles with this type of thing, that's why Dad always dealt with it before. Mum is a no-nonsense sort of woman. She works hard and expects other people to do the same. She wouldn't have time to listen to the entire Lia saga.

"I'm OK," I tell her. "There was no fight. I just felt sick and needed to get out of school. I should have gone to the medical room. I'm sorry."

"You could have managed the rest of the day, surely?" she replies. "You didn't puke, did you?"

"No. I was fine."

"Well, no more skiving off." She sighs. "I know you're struggling with Richie being here. But I don't need you acting up. This is a new start for us. You just need to open your mind to it."

I sniff and open up my magazine again. The page falls open at an article on some lame pop singer that I've barely heard of, but I pretend to be really interested.

"Please just give Richie a try," Mum says. "He's not your dad, he's not even trying to be. But he wants to get along with you. Is that OK?"

I shrug. "OK. Whatever."

Just don't expect us to be best mates or anything.

"Are you sure there's nothing else you want to tell me?" Mum asks.

I look up. Try to hold eye contact, because I've heard that's a sign you are telling the truth. "Mum – I'm fine."

She nods. "OK." She pauses, then adds, "So are you seeing your dad today, then?"

My cheeks burn. My dad ... She talks about him like he's a stranger to her now. Someone detached and foreign. She loved him once. Does she even remember?

"Yeah, I'm meeting him in a few hours," I tell her. "We're going to the game."

"He has tickets? Are you sure?" Mum frowns.

"Yes. Of course I am. We've been talking about it all week."

Mum shakes her head. "Funny how he finds money when he wants to."

I glare up at her. "He wants to take me out, Mum."

"Yes. Yes, of course. Well – I hope you enjoy it."

I watch as she leaves the room. It is all too easy. Weirdly, I wish she had pushed me a bit more, really pressed me to tell the truth. Now I long to shout after her:

"*No, Mum! I'm not OK. I feel really stressed. Really anxious.*"

"*Help me, Mum. Come back, talk to me.*"

But of course I say nothing.

I leave a note in my room. I put it on my pillow.
It's short and to the point:

> *Staying at Dad's for a bit. Speak to you*
> *soon x*

On the way out, I pass Kayla on the stairs. I have
to shove my bag behind my back so she doesn't
see it, but part of me doesn't even care if she
does. What business is it of hers anyway?

She reaches out and touches my arm.

"Poppy, I saw—" Kayla starts.

She's talking too loudly – the door to the
living room is wide open. I don't want anyone
else hearing what happened.

I rush past her, shoving her a bit. "I'm OK," I
tell her.

"Poppy ..."

I turn. Kayla's eyes are wide, her face
concerned. She looks like she is going to head

back down towards me, but I can't face that. I don't want her pity.

I can't think of anything worse.

"Just leave me alone," I hiss.

And I rush out of the front door, my bag bumping heavily against my side.

The match starts at three o'clock. Dad told me to meet him by the newsagent down the end of the road that leads to the stadium. We arranged to be here forty minutes before the game starts, just to be sure. This is the shop where we always stock up on match-day essentials – bottles of Coke, sucky sweets and a big bag of crisps to share. If Dad is feeling flush, he'll buy us burgers in the stadium when we go inside. I'm hoping that he is, as I'm already starving, having skipped breakfast to avoid another awkward conversation with Richie.

A mixture of excitement and nerves trickles through me. I love match days. I love spending them with Dad. These are golden days, something we rarely do any more, which makes it so much more precious.

I just can't wait to get in there, to be absorbed in the game and forget about everything else for a while.

I look at my watch and I see that fifteen minutes have passed already. There is still no sign of Dad. I check my phone, but there is nothing. No missed calls. No messages. An ache starts inside of me, right in the centre of my belly. I start to feel sick.

There is a swell of a crowd drifting past me down the main street towards the ground. Some people are chanting. Scarves and drinks are being waved in the air. I love the noise, the atmosphere. I want to be amongst them. Walking fast, singing and shouting. But I'm not. I'm outside looking in.

I'm not part of this.

He must be on his way. He must just be held up.

I sit on the small wall that runs alongside the shop. I always used to sit here while Dad was inside buying our goodies and his cigarettes. He would take too long and I'd end up kicking the bricks in frustration.

Now I am doing the same thing again – watching as the dust crumbles and falls on the pavement in rusty sprinkles.

I check my watch again. It's nearly three. Dad wouldn't be this late; he's never normally this late. He knows how important it is to get in there before the game starts.

I hear a distant roar as the whistle blows and the match begins. The ache inside me is deeper now and the tiny hole that was inside my stomach has opened up fully into a big gaping wound.

Reality sweeps me up in its cold, cruel grip. He's not coming.

I pick up my bag and start walking.

Chapter Nine

Dad took me to my first game when I was six years old. We'd both been so excited. I remember I kept running around the living room, full of energy, dragging my new scarf behind me like a trailing kite. Dad had even bought me the new season's shirt and I was wearing it proudly, even though it itched me like mad.

Mum didn't want to come. Football has never been her sort of thing. She finds it too loud and shouty. I think she was half expecting me to be the same. I remember her whispering in my ear as we went to leave: *"If you get bored, just tell Dad. He'll bring you straight back. He won't mind."*

I shook my head, certain even then that this was going to be perfect. Dad took my small hand in his and we strolled down the road. He taught me the songs to chant – the ones that weren't rude – and reminded me of the names of the players. When we got to the main street, the crowd suddenly grew in size, and Dad swept me high onto his shoulders so that I wouldn't get lost or scared. From up there, on my knobbly ridge, I could see right over the heads of the other fans. I was bobbing up and down with the rest of them, like a buoy out at sea. I looked up and I swear it felt like I could have touched the clouds – they seemed so close.

"*Are you OK?*" Dad had asked me, holding my legs tight.

"*Yes,*" I said, blinking at the perfect blue of the sky. "*I feel like a giant.*"

Because I did. I felt tall, powerful and so very, very lucky.

My dad had been the cause of that.

My dad.

And now where is he?

*

I walk fast, not really sure where I want to go. All I know for certain is that I need to get away from the noise of the stadium. I want no reminders that I should be in there with them. Not out here. Alone.

And I don't want to go home. That would be the worst thing. Mum would be sympathetic of course, but part of her would be smug. She always said that Dad was unreliable and untrustworthy. This just proved her right.

But this was the first time he'd let me down badly.

Yes, there had been other times. Especially when Mum and Dad were still together. Dad would often make promises about taking us out for the day, or coming home early and doing something special. It used to upset both Mum and me when he'd forget. When he chose to go down the pub instead. Sometimes I used to think he preferred being in the pub than at home with us.

But when Mum kicked Dad out, he told me he had changed. He was trying. He told me it was going to be different this time. He was going to put me first.

I snort. What a joke. And I was an idiot to believe him.

I find myself at the bus stop. I dig in my pocket – the loose change I pull out will get me into town. When the bus pulls up next to me, I automatically step on. Then I head to a seat at the back and press my body up against the side of the vehicle. It's not full in here at all, just a couple of older women chatting near the doors and a man sitting in front. I'm relieved. The last thing I need is to see someone from school.

I pull out my phone and check it again. There's still nothing from Dad, but there is a missed call from Mum and a message:

Call me.

I ignore it. I don't want to deal with her right now. I wonder whether Kayla has grassed up about the video and now Mum will want to discuss the entire situation.

Or maybe she has already found the note in my room. She probably thinks I'm with Dad right now. That I'll be with him for the next couple of days.

Well, that's not going to happen now ...

I hook up to the bus's wi-fi and go online. I don't know why, but I feel the need to watch Lia's video again. This time it doesn't sting as much. I know what's coming, I guess. I'm more prepared. This time I feel more like an observer.

I watch again as I'm filmed hitting the ground, as Charlotte comes up behind me, her snaky smile spreading across her face. I watch as that drink is poured over my head, slowly and deliberately.

I look down at the comments. There are loads more, but to my surprise more angry messages have been added. Fliss is the first one. I could totally hug her right now.

This is out of order. How old are you?
Take this off, you sick bitches.

And it looks as if Fliss has started a trend. More supportive messages have been written in the last few hours.

This is pathetic ...

Poor Poppy – you guys are bang out of order.

Yeah – nice one! You're just making yourselves look dumb here.

Low move ...

Wipe this now.

I blink, hardly able to believe it. They can see. People can see Charlotte and Lia for what they are. Not some cool, funny girls – but just pathetic nobodies.

I move back to the video again. Without thinking too much about it, I save it to my device.

I realise I'm not upset any more. Not about anything.

I'm just really, really angry.

Chapter Ten

I get off the bus at the last stop in town. It's a quieter area, mainly full of cafes and charity shops. As I walk along, I count out the last of my change. I have four pounds, which will buy me a drink and the bus ride back home.

Back home. I shiver at the thought.

I'm still clutching my stupid bag. The one I'd packed, hoping I could stay at Dad's. How dumb had I been? As if he'd want me around, getting in the way. And how would it have helped anything anyway? Sitting in Dad's tiny bedsit would hardly sort out all my problems. Only I can do that. What would I have done? Sat there and watched him drinking? How would that solve anything?

I can't keep running away from what is happening in my life.

I walk into the nearest cafe and order myself a Coke. Then I sit back in a chair by the window and turn off my phone. I need to shut out the noise for a bit.

I guess I have a lot of thinking to do.

A few hours later, I am back on the bus. My head feels a bit clearer, but I'm dead tired. I reckon I would sleep for a month straight if I could.

I decide to walk back home via the park. I know there's a risk that I'll bump into Lia and her lot, but weirdly I'm not worried about that any more. Let them say their worst. I know I have support now. I know that I've done nothing wrong. I'm not going to hide away like a scared animal. Not any more.

I've done nothing wrong.

I'm passing the main play area, past the swings and zipwire, when I hear my name being called. My skin prickles. I pause, unsure, and then I turn.

I'm expecting to see Lia. Or Charlotte. Or any one of those girls grinning back at me, ready for the next fight. But it's not them.

It's Kayla.

She walks slowly towards me. I notice she has less make-up on than normal. Her face looks pale and her hair is pulled back into a messy ponytail.

"Where have you been?" Kayla asks, coming up next to me. She touches my arm lightly. "We've all been worried sick. We've been looking everywhere. This was my last stop."

"I ..." I shake my head. I'm not sure what to tell her. It seems so lame to admit that I was riding a bus, sitting in a cafe. "I just needed some time alone," I say finally.

Kayla smiles. "Yeah, I get that. It's been pretty rough for you, eh?" She squeezes my arm. It's such a gentle action it makes me want to cry. "Your mum found your note," Kayla adds. "Saying you were going to stay at your dad's for a bit. And then when your dad turned up at ours—"

"He turned up at home?" I say, stepping back, confused. "He was meant to meet me before the match. He never showed up."

Kayla frowns a bit. "I heard him and your mum shouting about it. From what I could make out, he had too much to drink last night. He lost his phone and his wallet. By the time he got to the house, it was too late – you'd left."

I half laugh. "So Dad was out getting wasted when I was trying to call him? When I was asking for help?" I snort. "Why do I never learn?"

"I'm sorry," Kayla says. "But you have us as well, remember. You need to talk to us too."

"But my dad ..."

I can't finish. How can I explain to Kayla that it is my dad who normally fixes things, that it's my dad I normally turn to? But then I look at Kayla and see that she's nodding gently.

"I get it, Poppy. I do. Remember it's been me and my dad for a long time. Ever since my mum died. He's done everything for me and he's always tried to be there. But it's been tough at times – like I'm guessing it's tough for your dad at the moment. But we got through it and so can he."

"I think Dad's struggling," I mutter.

"Maybe. And you are too. But I think it will get easier for him." Kayla shifts on the spot. "My dad was so worried. He thought you might have run away. He thought all of this was somehow his fault. Dad really cares about you, Poppy. He just wants you to be happy. Everyone does."

"Is my dad still there?" I ask.

Kayla smiles. "Yes! They've been worried sick about you." She pauses. "I have to ring them. Your mum and dad are out in the car looking for you and my dad stayed at home in case you came back."

I watch, feeling awkward as she pulls out her phone and calls Richie. She turns away from me, but I can still hear a few words that she says. She tells him that I'm OK and that we are coming back now. I hear her tell him that she loves him.

"He's so relieved," she says softly. "He's going to call your mum now. They'll be there when we get home."

My skin prickles. "They are going to be so mad at me."

"I don't think they will be. We were all just worried about you." She touches my arm. "It's not all bad, you know. Your parents have been talking. I think they want to sort stuff out. Make things easier for you."

"All of this ..." I say. "It's just so hard ..." I can't get out the right words.

"I know. It's hard for all of us. It's hard for me moving into a brand-new house and starting over. It's hard for my dad trying to fit in. It's hard for your mum trying to keep the peace ..."

"I'm sorry," I say.

Kayla leans forward and then sweeps me up in a hug. It's so unexpected it makes me gasp. As she pulls away, I see that there are tears in her eyes.

"Your mum makes my dad so happy," Kayla says. "There was a time I never thought that could happen again. Dad was in such a bad place once, I thought I'd never see him smile."

I stare back at her. "Really? I didn't know."

"Sure. After Mum died, it was like something in Dad died too. Even I couldn't make him feel good again." Kayla pauses, draws a shaky breath. "I'm just so thankful to your mum. I want this to work out. For all of us."

I nod. "I do too."

She takes my hand in hers and squeezes it. "You're not alone, Poppy," Kayla says. "Just remember that. You have me now. We have each other."

We walk back home together. It feels strangely comfortable, as if it's always been like this. I'd seen Kayla as this distant, unapproachable person, when in fact nothing could be further from the truth. As we talk, I realise how laid-back Kayla is, almost geeky. She's totally easy to talk to.

"I have to confront Lia," I tell her as we walk down the road. "I have to sort out all of this mess. She can't get away with it."

"No," Kayla agrees. "She can't. I've been raging about it to my year group. They're not impressed. They think Lia is pathetic. In fact, by the end of school yesterday, everybody was feeling the same. That's what I was trying to tell you this morning."

"Oh ..." I pause. "So most people in school have seen the video, then?" I can feel my skin redden.

Kayla flaps out her hands. "And?" she says. "So what? It doesn't make you look bad at all. You just fall over and have some bitch dump a drink on your head. If anything, you come off as being dignified and calm. It's those shrieking, childish cows who did this to you that are getting roasted."

I grin. "Really?"

Kayla nods. "Yep. And, just for your information, Jamie is going to see Lia this weekend to tell her to her face what a child she is being. Lia was never going out with Jamie anyway. He snogged her once and she got obsessed and started making stuff up. It's driving Jamie mad. She is not coming off well here at all."

"OK," I say. "Well, I'm feeling a bit better."

"So you should." Kayla smiles. "I've not even told you the best bit. One of Lia's idiot friends uploaded the video onto the school's social channel. So now the head knows about it. From what I've heard, Lia and Charlotte are going to be in serious trouble on Monday."

"At least it might be over now."

"I believe in karma," Kayla says. "And in this case, Lia is certainly going to get hers."

Chapter Eleven

They are all sitting in the living room, waiting for me.

Mum, Dad and Richie.

I don't like this. It feels beyond weird. Dad just looks wrong, on the sofa next to Richie. How could that even be? It wasn't so long ago that Dad would have been lying out on there, happily watching TV or reading. How did things change so fast? Now Dad's perched on the edge of the seat, looking like he wants to be anywhere else but here.

Dad jumps up as I walk in. "Poppy. Thank God!"

Mum runs over to me. She pulls me into a hug. "You had me so worried," she says into my hair.

Richie walks towards me and lightly taps me on the shoulder. "Good to see you back in one piece," he says. I pull myself away from Mum and smile weakly at Richie. I never noticed before how tired he looks.

"Thanks," I say.

"I'll leave you guys to talk," Richie says, and slowly guides Kayla out of the room. She flashes me a "see, it's OK" glance as she leaves. They close the door behind them.

I flop down on the sofa, exhausted. My eyes scan the clock. It's nearly nine now. I've been out of the house for seven hours.

"You didn't need to worry," I tell them.

"You had your phone turned off," Mum says softly. "You weren't replying to us. I knew you were planning to meet your dad and then when he showed up here, I panicked."

"I know," I say. "I'm sorry. I just needed to get away for a bit."

"And the note?" Mum asks.

I shrug. "I just wanted to be with Dad for a while, that's all." I look at Dad straight in the eyes. "But that's not going to work out, is it?"

Dad seems smaller somehow. He rubs his face with his hand and says, "I'm so sorry, Poppy. I let you down. I keep letting you down. I keep messing stuff up."

"But you're sorting yourself out now, aren't you?" Mum says firmly to him.

Dad nods. "I can't carry on like this. It's not fair on any of us. I'm going to get a steady job. Get help with the drinking ..."

He trails off.

The drinking. Of course I knew he drank quite a bit when he lived here. It caused rows between him and Mum, but I never thought it was that bad. Dad was always happy when he was drunk. If anything, he was more fun.

But looking at him now, I can see the mess he's become. His clothes are shabby. His hair needs cutting. His skin is grey. I can see what Mum can see.

What Mum has seen for years.

"I need to grow up," Dad tells me softly. I notice how he has deep shadows under his eyes. How his cheeks are sunken slightly. "I can't keep on acting like a kid."

"I just want you to keep your promises," I say. "I thought today—"

"I know. I know." Dad hangs his head. "I should have called you. I should have told you that I didn't have the money for tickets. But I left it too late and then I lost my phone down the pub. I tried to get here as soon as I could. I tried to stop you going."

"I was left waiting for you," I say.

"I know and I'm so very sorry." Dad looks up and I see tears are glistening in his eyes. "I will make it up to you."

"It's a storm, Dad, remember?" I say, my voice trembling. "It will pass."

Despite it all, he's still my dad.

And I need him back.

*

After Dad leaves, Mum sits with me. For a while we just sit in silence; sometimes she strokes my back. Then, finally, Mum speaks.

"I should have been more honest with you, Poppy. I'm sorry. I just didn't want you hating your dad."

"I thought you kicked him out for no reason. Replaced him with Richie because he suited you better."

Mum snorts. "No. Not at all. Richie had been a friend for some time. We used to talk when I was on shift and he'd make me laugh, take my mind off things – you know? Life was so difficult here with your dad. We just resented each other. He wanted to be out drinking with his mates, gambling, watching footie. I wanted him to be more responsible. It couldn't work." Mum's voice breaks a bit. "But I did try. I tried for a long time."

"Are you happy now?" I ask her.

She squeezes me. "Yes, yes, I am. I have a man who loves and respects me. It's so important, Poppy. I have someone who makes me feel good about myself. Who listens to me."

Mum sighs gently as she strokes my back once again. "I just need you to be happy again. That's all I really want."

I lean up against her.

"I'll try, Mum."

I'll try.

It's quiet in my room. I've read the messages on my phone and thankfully it's all calmed down. Lia has removed the video. I don't know why; I don't even care. All I know is that the people who are contacting me are on my side.

The last message was from Jamie. It simply said:

Lia promises to leave you alone now. I've had words. Respect to you for handling it so well.

A warm feeling passes through me. I feel like I've achieved something, no matter how small. I didn't let Lia win.

I turn my phone off. I don't need to read any more.

There is a knock at my door and I'm startled. It's pretty late now. I guess it will be Kayla maybe, wanting a chat. Or even Mum checking up on me.

I don't expect Richie. He stands by the door, looking a bit awkward. He's still wearing a too-loud shirt and his smile is still cheesy. But I like the fact that he is being respectful and not coming in.

I walk over and ask, "What's up?"

Richie's holding his phone. "I just want to show you something. I hope you don't mind?"

I shrug. *Go on.*

Richie coughs. "I was thinking about your dad, how he really wanted to take you to a game but he couldn't. It didn't seem fair somehow. You two deserve some time together. I know I'd hate it if I couldn't be with Kayla." He coughs again. "So I bought this for you. Call it an early Christmas present."

I look down at his phone. For a second, I can't believe what I'm seeing.

"A season ticket?" I say. "For two? Richie, I don't—"

"Please," he interrupts. "Please accept it. It's my gift. I want to help. This way you and your dad can go to every game together, if you want to."

"But Dad?"

I'm not even sure he'd accept this.

"He can pay me back when he can, if he wants to. I got the tickets at a stupidly cheap price." Richie grins again, flashing those too-white teeth. "I cashed in a few favours."

"I don't know what to say."

I really don't.

"You don't need to say anything," Richie says gently. "I'm just glad I can help."

Before I can stop myself, I sweep Richie into a hug. "Thank you," I say. "This means so much to me."

And honestly, I really mean it.

Richie will never be my dad, and I can see now that he's not even trying to be. But he's the man who makes my mum happy.

Richie's trying to make me happy too. And that's a big deal.

So I've got to stop fighting and begin accepting.

This is a new start for all of us.

Richie moving in was a D-Day of sorts. But not in a bad way. *In a good way*. The war is over. The rebuilding now begins.

Our books are tested
for children and young people by
children and young people.

Thanks to everyone who consulted on
a manuscript for their time and effort in
helping us to make our books better
for our readers.